Dr. Ruth
Talks to Kids

Dr. Ruth Talks to Kids

Where You Came From, How Your Body Changes, and What Sex Is All About

Dr. Ruth Westheimer

Illustrated by Diane deGroat

Macmillan Publishing Company   New York

Maxwell Macmillan Canada   Toronto

Maxwell Macmillan International
New York   Oxford   Singapore   Sydney

Dr. Westheimer wishes to thank Ben Yagoda for the writing skill and sensitivity that made this cooperative venture possible and pleasurable. She also wishes to thank Gigi Simeone, Mr. Yagoda's wife, and his two daughters, Elizabeth and Maria. In addition, she thanks Macmillan editor Beverly Reingold and editorial assistant Josette Haddad for their contributions. For their very helpful critique of the manuscript, she thanks Harvey R. Greenberg, M.D., Clinical Professor of Psychiatry at New York's Albert Einstein College of Medicine, and Jacob Mayron, M.D., Associate Professor of Obstetrics and Gynecology, New York University Medical Center. Finally, she thanks her family, David Adler, Rabbi Leonard Kravitz, Rabbi Robert Lehman, Pierre Lehu, Professor Louis Lieberman, and Maria Cuadrado.

Macmillan Publishing Company is part of the
Maxwell Communication Group of Companies.
Macmillan Publishing Company
866 Third Avenue, New York, NY 10022
Maxwell Macmillan Canada, Inc.
1200 Eglinton Avenue East, Suite 200
Don Mills, Ontario M3C 3N1
First edition
Printed in the United States of America

10   9   8   7   6   5   4   3   2   1
The text of this book is set in 12 point ITC Garamond Light.
The illustrations are rendered in pencil.

Library of Congress Cataloging-in-Publication Data
Westheimer, Ruth K. (Ruth Karola), date.
Dr. Ruth talks to kids : where you came from, how
your body changes, and what sex is all about /
Ruth Westheimer ; illustrated by Diane deGroat. — 1st ed.
p.   cm.
Includes bibliographical references and index.
Summary: The noted sex therapist discusses the physical and
psychological changes that occur when a child grows up.
ISBN 0-02-792532-3
1. Sex instruction for children. [1. Sex instruction for children.]
I. De Groat, Diane, ill.   II. Title.
HQ53.W47   1993   306.7'07—dc20   92-11397

To my grandson, Ari, a delightful boy,
and to all the children of my family
and friends—the future generation

Now therefore, O ye children,
hearken unto me . . .
—Proverbs, chapter 5, verse 7

Hear instruction, and be wise . . .
—Proverbs, chapter 8, verse 33

Contents

Introduction

I have a confession to make. When I was seven or eight years old, I thought that the stork brought babies. I was an only child, and I was lonely. So I decided to leave two lumps of sugar outside my window for the stork. Maybe then he would bring me a brother or sister.

Guess what? It didn't work.

I wasn't the only kid in Germany, where I was born and lived until I was ten, who had that silly idea about storks. It was the answer lots of German parents gave when their children asked, "Where do babies come from?" In other countries parents tell different stories. In France parents say that babies are found under cabbage leaves.

And in America, where everything is modern and up-to-date, children are informed that babies come from the hospital. I know that's what my son thought when he was a little boy. Every time we drove by a hospital, he would shout, "Let's go in and pick up a baby!"

The point is this: When it comes to questions about where babies come from, and the way our bodies change as we're growing up, and what sex is all about, very few people know all the right answers. I'll tell you why this is the case. In our society, sexuality is treated as a very private matter. This is a good thing—would you want the whole world to be watching when you're kissing your boyfriend or girlfriend?—but it has some bad results. One of them is that people are often very uncomfortable talking about sex. And if they can't talk about it, how can they find out about it?

Even your parents would probably rather discuss baseball, or your report card, or the weather. If you insist, sometimes they'll tell you what you want to know. But usually they'll get embarrassed and flustered and their faces will get red. Maybe they'll stammer out a few facts.

Your friends probably aren't much better. They might act as if they know it all, but what they're likely to end up proving is how little they know. Meanwhile, you're liable to get wrong information, and sometimes no information at all.

This is really too bad. Over the next few years, your life is going to change in ways you can't even imagine. You'll develop new likes and dislikes, new friends, new thoughts and ideas—and a new body. The boys will start to shave. They'll get muscles. Their voices will suddenly deepen. The girls will develop breasts and wider hips. They'll start to menstruate. And both boys and girls will find they have a strong interest in sexual subjects. These changes should make kids feel *great*. They mean that a whole new, exciting world is opening up. But if kids don't understand what's going on, the changes can make them feel bewildered, even frightened. Lack of information could also result in their doing things that they don't really want to, or aren't ready for yet.

And that's the reason for this book. If you keep reading, you're going to find information that will help you understand and cope with and enjoy all the changes as they come. We're going to talk about things that you might feel are too private to discuss with anyone else. But since these things don't make me feel the least bit uncomfortable, there's no reason why you should feel that way, either.

So put a Do Not Disturb sign outside your bedroom, close the door, turn off your radio, and sit down in your favorite chair. You and I are going to have a good talk.

1

Your Body

In the movie business there is an expression, *cut to the chase*. It means to skip the dull parts of a film and get right away to what people are really interested in—a car chase. (*I* don't find car chases very interesting, so I guess it's a good thing I'm not in the movie business.)

I'm going to cut to the chase right now. Remember I said that sexuality is a private matter in our society? Maybe the best example of that is the fact that when we're around other people, certain parts of our bodies—the sexual parts—are *always* covered with clothes. So if you're a girl, you might not know exactly what's under a boy's bathing suit, and if you're a boy, you might not know what's under a girl's.

Of course, you probably know more than I did when I was a little girl. In those days, there was no such thing as an "anatomically correct" doll. When I went to shop for dolls for my daughter, I was surprised to find that some of them were built just like real people, down to the last detail.

One thing that *did* exist when I was young was curiosity. When I was ten years old, my parents sent me to a children's home in Switzerland because World War II was about to begin; I lived there until I was sixteen. The boys and girls lived in different parts of the building. I remember a group of us girls peeking into the boys' bathroom when they were taking showers. We thought we were getting away with something, but when I look back on it today, I'm pretty sure they knew we were peeking.

Anyway, in case you don't know exactly how things are set up for the opposite sex, or if you think you do but aren't quite sure, I'm going to give you a quick guided tour.

Let's start with boys. Until they reach *puberty*—which means the age at which a child's body starts to become more like a grown-up's—they're built much like girls, except that between their legs is something called a *penis.* The penis is an organ that's attached a few inches below the belly button. It hangs down and looks a little bit like a finger (sometimes a very short finger, sometimes a long one) without any fingernail, and with a small opening at the end. The opening is where the urine comes out.

Some boys' penises are *circumcised.* This means that, probably shortly after they were born, the layer of skin that covers the end of the penis—the *foreskin*—was cut away. Parents usually decide to circumcise their boy babies either for religious or for what they believe to be health reasons (although all doctors don't agree whether those health reasons are valid). But circumcised and uncircumcised penises work exactly the same way. The only thing boys should remember if they were not circumcised is that it's important, maybe once a week or so, to push back the foreskin and wash the head of the penis.

Between the penis and the rest of the body is the *scrotum.* This is the loose, wrinkled pouch of skin that holds two *testes,* oval-shaped internal organs that, as any boy knows, are very sensitive to pain.

The penis is pretty amazing. For one thing, a boy urinates through it. And, since it can be aimed, a boy can stand up when he goes to the bathroom. Another amazing thing is the way the penis undergoes an *erection*. Normally soft, it sometimes gets hard and longer and sticks straight out. This can happen when a boy rubs his penis or it rubs against something; it can happen when he has a strong urge to urinate, and it can happen for no reason at all. (By the way, one slang term for an erection, a *boner,* is misleading: There are no bones in the penis, and an erection happens because of a quick flow of blood into it.)

Now for the girls. Their bathing suits cover their chests, but until they reach puberty, their chests are exactly the same as boys'—two nipples, one on either side.

In the place where boys have a penis, however, things are completely different. Girls have a *vulva,* which looks like a pair of lips, running up and down instead of side to side. In the crack between them, and invisible from the outside, is the *vagina,* a barrel-shaped opening. Inside the vagina is a thin membrane called the *hymen,* which partly closes the opening.

Girls urinate through the *urethra,* a thin opening inside the vulva, just above the vagina. It can't be aimed, so they have to go to the bathroom sitting down.

Just above the urethra is the *clitoris,* a small knob of tissue that is very sensitive to the touch.

Your body is always changing, but never so much as during the process called puberty, which can begin when you're as young as eight or nine or as old as sixteen or seventeen. Usually it starts when you're somewhere in between. Anyway, with puberty, things change. Oh, boy, do they change. And many of the changes, physical and emotional, have to do in one way or another with sex.

Sex can't be summed up even in a whole book, much less a single paragraph, but a basic part of it is an activity called *sexual intercourse.*

During it, a man inserts his erect penis into a woman's vagina. Sometimes, as a result of sexual intercourse, the woman becomes pregnant, and after nine months or so, she has a baby. That's how you began, and if you ever have children, that's how they will begin, too.

Changes During Puberty: Girls

The ways in which your body changes during puberty make it possible for you to have a baby. Now let's talk about these changes. Boys and girls both have a sort of invisible alarm clock inside their bodies. But it doesn't ring. Instead, at just the right time, it tells different glands to start producing a lot of *hormones* and to send them through your bloodstream. Hormones are chemicals that influence both the way the body develops and the way people feel.

In girls, the first new development will usually be the growth of breasts. At first the area surrounding the nipple gets larger and pushes out in a small mound. Over the next few years, it continues to grow, and the nipple and surrounding area—the *areola*—develop, as well. At the same time, a girl's hips and buttocks get larger, so that the shape of her body begins to take on the well-known "hourglass" figure.

The biological reason for breasts is simple: After a woman gives birth, special glands inside her breasts produce milk for the baby. Also, the breast—especially the area around the nipple—is known as an *erogenous zone,* an area of the body that's very sensitive, and that feels good when it is touched. Some other erogenous zones are the clitoris, the earlobe, the back of the neck, and the upper thigh (the last three of which are erogenous zones for boys, too).

In America, much more so than in other countries I've lived in or learned about, people are fascinated by breasts. You can tell by all the slang words used here for breasts, by the way people get embarrassed and giggly when the subject comes up, even by the way shirts and dresses and bathing suits are designed to make them the center of attention.

Because of all this hubbub, girls are usually very self-conscious about their breasts. They want to know when their breasts will grow, how they will look and feel, what size and shape they will be, and what the sensation of having them will be. I'm sorry to have to say this, but I don't know the answers to these questions: Breasts can begin to grow when a girl is as young as eight or nine or as old as fourteen or fifteen, and there are as many different types of them as there are women.

But that's actually good news. It means that whatever your breasts look like, they're probably normal. Small breasts function just as well, and are as attractive to boys, as big ones; big breasts don't make you clumsy or unattractive. Of course, I know that I can say this until I'm blue in the face, and once your breasts develop, you'll still worry about them. They're too small. They're too big. One is bigger than the other. They have a funny shape.

I speak from good authority about this because I developed breasts at an early age. Since I've always been short, they were very noticeable when I was thirteen or fourteen and they had grown to their full size. I was *very* self-conscious, especially after a woman who worked in the children's home saw me one day and made a cupping motion around her breasts, as if to say how big mine were. I'm *still* furious at her. I thought something was wrong with me. It took me a long time to realize that something was wrong with *her.*

At some point you will probably want to start wearing a bra. Especially if you do have larger breasts, you may find that the support the bra gives makes you more comfortable. If you're active in sports, you'll probably want to wear a special athletic bra.

But you can wait awhile after your breasts begin to develop before you get your first bra. In other words, I don't believe in training bras. I remember when my daughter (who's now married and the mother of the most gorgeous little boy in the world) told me she wanted a training bra. I said, "Training for what?"

There are other physical changes that come along with puberty. Girls often get a growth spurt, where they shoot up a few inches in a year or two, and their voices get a little bit deeper. They also start to grow body hair—under their arms, around their genitals (this is known as *pubic hair*), and usually on their arms and legs. As with so many other things, different cultures have different attitudes about this. After I left the children's home in Switzerland, I lived on a kibbutz in Israel. There *nobody* shaved her legs or under her arms. In America, of course, most women do. You should do whatever makes you feel comfortable.

The changes we've been talking about so far have one thing in common: You can see them. But just as many changes take place inside the body. These changes help to explain *menstruation,* a long word that describes something rather simple that happens a year or two after a girl begins to grow breasts: Every month or so, for three or four days or maybe a week, a little bit of a bloody discharge will come out of her vagina.

The reason for menstruation—which is also sometimes called a girl's period—is a little more complicated. You need to know that inside a girl's abdomen, from the moment she's born, are two small organs called *ovaries,* about the size and shape of unshelled almonds. They contain thousands of tiny *ova,* otherwise known as egg cells.

When a girl reaches puberty, her body begins to perform a regular series of procedures that will continue for the next thirty to forty years. At the beginning of the cycle, one or the other of the ovaries pushes an ovum into a passageway next to it called the *fallopian tube.*

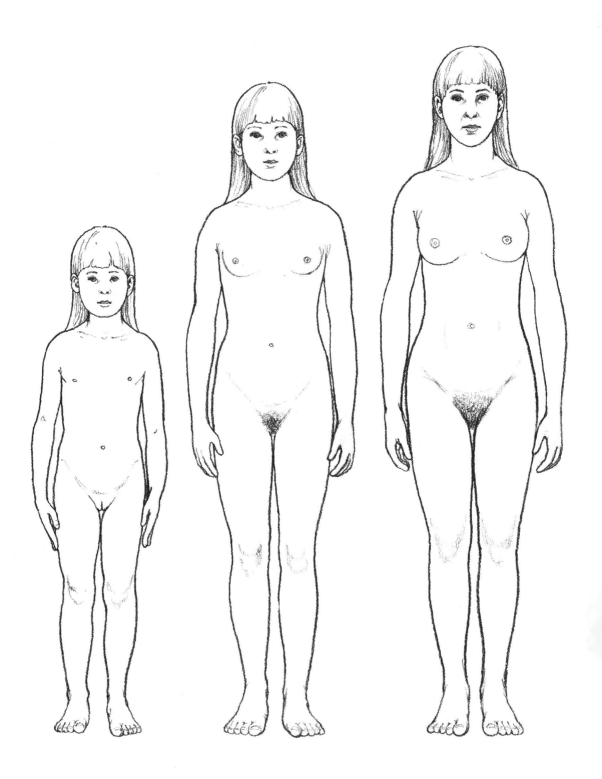

This is called *ovulation*. If a woman has sexual intercourse with a man close to this time, a *sperm* cell from the man may enter the egg and *fertilize* it. If it is fertilized, it travels to the thick lining of the *uterus*, a pear-shaped organ, about three inches long, that's connected to the vagina. The lining protects the egg and nourishes it as it begins to grow into an embryo, which turns into a fetus, which develops into a baby.

If the egg *isn't* fertilized, the body doesn't need it anymore, and it disintegrates. There's no need for the lining of the uterus, either, so the body begins to shed the blood and tissue that the lining is made of. These collect at the bottom of the uterus, then dribble out the vagina. This is menstruation.

Then the whole cycle starts over, and the lining is rebuilt only to be sloughed away again. By the way, while each woman generally has cycles of the same length, cycles vary in length from woman to

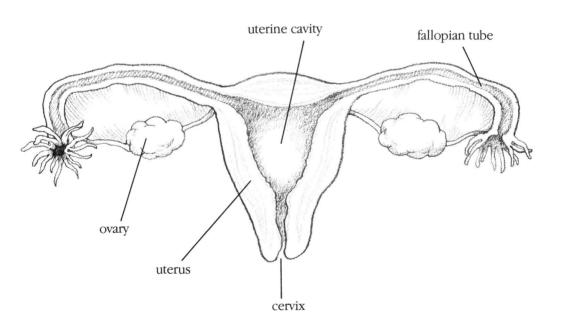

uterine cavity

fallopian tube

ovary

uterus

cervix

woman. They run anywhere from twenty to forty days; the average cycle is twenty-eight days.

Different girls begin to menstruate, or have their *periods,* at different ages. The range is generally between ten and seventeen, and most girls start between twelve and fifteen. Sometimes a girl will have her first period and then not have another one for several months. Other girls have their second period just two weeks after the first. Most find that after they've been menstruating for two or three years, their periods come very regularly.

Sometimes a woman will find that, even though it's the right time of month for her period, she isn't menstruating. There could be a number of reasons for this, including stress, gaining or losing a lot of weight, or pregnancy (if a woman is pregnant, then the fertilized egg needs the uterine lining and the lining stays in the body). Otherwise, the pattern will continue until a woman is somewhere between the ages of forty-five and fifty-five. That's when the body goes through menopause, a whole series of changes. One of them is the end of menstruation, which means that a woman can't get pregnant anymore.

When you menstruate, the blood and tissue must be absorbed by a tampon or a sanitary napkin. You may have heard about these things. A tampon is a plug that fits inside the vagina. Learning to insert it takes some practice, but once you get the hang of it, it's easy. Sanitary napkins are pads that have adhesive on the bottom so that they stick to underwear. You wear tampons or napkins throughout your period, changing them several times a day.

Which should you use? Well, it's *not* true, as some people seem to think, that girls shouldn't use tampons because a tampon will break the hymen. In reality, the hymen usually leaves a big enough opening so that you can fit a tampon in. Also, tampons have one big advantage over sanitary napkins: You can go swimming with them! Otherwise,

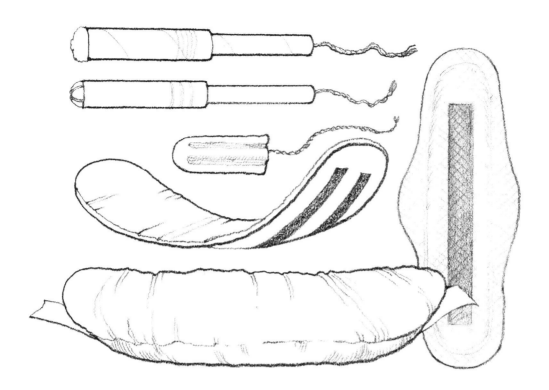

it's all a matter of personal choice. Your mother, your relatives, or your girlfriends can tell you what brands they like, and help you learn how to use them.

The start of menstruation is a big moment in a girl's life, and naturally girls react to it emotionally. Some can't wait for their periods to start. Others worry about what their periods will be like. They might have heard older girls refer to menstruation as "the curse"—a silly expression that has no basis in fact. Or they might have heard some of the myths that people used to believe about menstruation—that the blood comes from the brain, meaning girls and women can't think straight during their periods, or really crazy things, such as that if somebody eats food cooked by a menstruating woman, he or she will get sick. Or girls might just be scared of such a big change.

I know exactly how these girls feel: When you're used to being a little girl, it isn't easy to all of a sudden become a woman. It wasn't so long ago that you were a baby. Now it's possible for you to have one yourself. Just remember that starting to menstruate doesn't mean you're a grown-up. You're still a girl, and you can still act silly, or play with dolls, or cry sometimes.

Some girls are afraid that their periods will hurt. And it's true that some get cramps during their periods—a feeling that can range from a little tummy ache to a sharp pain. Some girls and women can experience headaches, backaches, or nausea. Others don't feel any discomfort, and may even find that they feel better and more energetic than usual during their periods. And if cramps are a problem, there are medicines that will help. Your doctor can recommend these.

Some girls and women experience changes in mood at the time of their periods, others do not. The other important thing to remember is that no one else can tell when you are menstruating. Usually the first period is very light, and you'll feel a sensation of wetness before there's any real secretion. So if you're with a group of people, you'll have time to excuse yourself and go to the bathroom for a sanitary napkin. (If you don't have one, just put some toilet paper inside your underpants for the moment.) From then on, more liquid will flow, but not much—the total over the course of the period is never more than about four tablespoons.

Also, remember that a girl will be able to predict pretty much when in the month her period is coming. As soon as it starts, she can wear a sanitary napkin or tampon, and continue with all her normal activities.

It was a little different when I was a girl. Tampons hadn't been invented yet, and we didn't have disposable sanitary napkins at the orphanage in Switzerland where I lived. So we used cloth ones and had to wash them by hand every night. And when I had my period, I *couldn't* go swimming with all the other children. Sometimes the boys teased me about it. I'm sure your parents often tell you that they had it rougher than you when they were growing up. Well, in this case, I did!

Whom should you tell when your period starts? That's entirely up to you. Some girls want to tell everybody they know. Others want to tell only their mothers. My advice is that you tell *someone,* if not your mother, then an older sister, or the school nurse, or a favorite aunt. They've gone through exactly the same thing, and they're sure to have some helpful words. Besides, all it really means is that you're growing up—good news that would really be selfish to keep to yourself. You might even want to throw yourself a party.

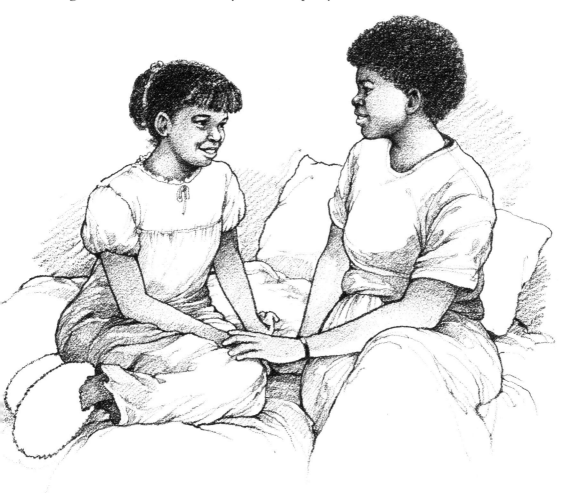

If you have any unusual problems with menstruation, your doctor may refer you to a *gynecologist*. This is a doctor who specializes in conditions that involve the female sex organs. She or he usually examines the vagina with an instrument called a *speculum*. The exam is not the most pleasant thing in the world, but it's not such a big deal, either, and if you can learn to relax (by taking deep breaths, for example), it will go much more comfortably than if your muscles are tense and tight.

At some point, even if you don't have a physical problem, you will begin to see a gynecologist about once a year. A woman continues to see a gynecologist throughout her whole life, and it's very important that there be a good relationship between doctor and patient. If you don't like or trust your gynecologist, by all means tell your parents. They'll help you find somebody new.

Changes During Puberty: Boys

I admit that I don't have personal experience when it comes to the changes a boy goes through. But I've been married for over thirty years and have had a son for twenty-nine. So I know something about the male child, teenager, and adult.

On the average, boys start to go through puberty later than girls—about two years later. The first changes you'll notice will be in your genitals, the area around your penis. Somewhere between the ages of ten and fifteen, you'll find that your testes and scrotum will be getting bigger, and that pubic hair will start to grow above and on either side of your penis. Within a year or so, the penis itself will grow, and most boys find that, at about the same time, they shoot up a couple of inches in height.

They also find that they have erections more than they used to. Sometimes they get one when they think about kissing a girl (and sometimes they get one when they *are* kissing a girl); sometimes they

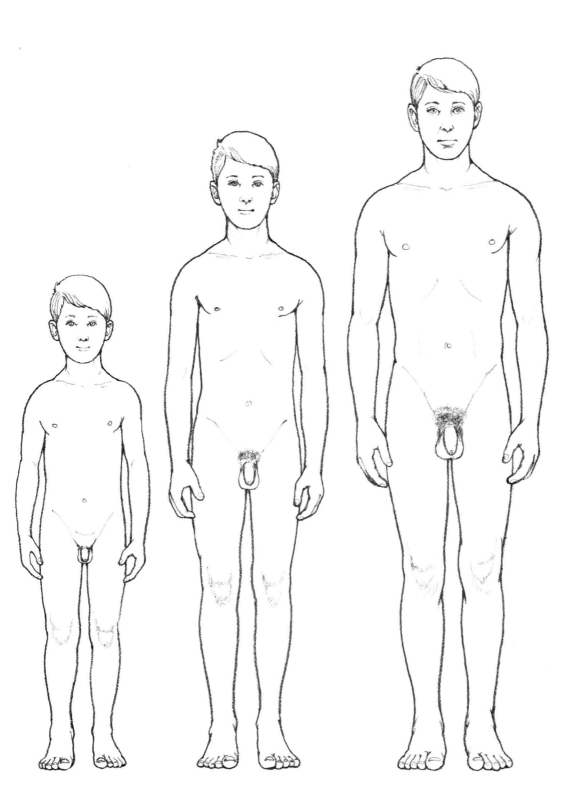

get one when they're nervous or excited; sometimes they get one when they're sitting in an uncomfortable position; sometimes they get one on waking up; and sometimes they get one for no reason at all. The erections usually go away after a few minutes. This is a problem only when you're in class and have to walk to the blackboard before those few minutes are up.

What do you do? Well, there's not much you *can* do. The panic you feel when you hear your name called out might make the erection go away all by itself. Maybe if you think about something really unpleasant, it will disappear. Otherwise, remember that erections aren't as noticeable (or uncomfortable) if you wear loose-fitting pants. And bear in mind that the teacher—whether a man or a woman—has seen this dozens of times before, and that no matter how much *you're* thinking about what's going on below your belt, your classmates have no reason to look there and probably won't even notice.

Every boy experiences these changes, but it's important to remember that there's no set timetable for them. Some fourteen- or fifteen-year-old boys don't have pubic hair yet. These late developers sometimes feel embarrassed in the locker room or shower at school. And too often their so-called friends make them feel even worse. At the children's home in Switzerland, I once overheard a group of boys making fun of a kid in this situation. Unfortunately, there's no way to respond to stupid cruelty like this. Just remember that it's only a matter of time before you're equipped like everybody else.

Anyway, boys are proud of their newly developed penises. Around this age, they sometimes get together in pairs or groups and play a game of "I'll show you mine and you show me yours." Sometimes they even touch each other's penises. There's absolutely nothing wrong with this, and it does *not* mean that the kids are *homosexual*. (Homosexuals are people sexually attracted to members of their own sex.)

Just as girls worry about the size and shape of their breasts, a lot of boys are very concerned about their penises. Again, there's no reason to be concerned. The average penis for the adult male is between two-and-a-half and four inches long, but many, many are shorter or longer than that. Some are thicker, some are thinner. Some are straight, some curve a little to one side or the other. So whatever yours is like, it's normal. And when the time comes to have sexual intercourse, the size of your penis doesn't have anything to do with how "good" at it you'll be, any more than the size of your finger does.

Speaking of your finger, if you think your penis is too small, your eyes may be playing tricks on you. Here's an experiment to show you what I mean. Stand up and, with your right arm hanging straight down, point your index finger at your right foot. Now look at your finger. Doesn't it seem shorter than it really is? That's because of an optical illusion called foreshortening. The same thing happens when you look down at your penis. To get a better idea of its length, look at it in a full-length mirror. I bet you'll be surprised.

Ready for more changes? About a year after pubic hair starts coming in, your larynx, otherwise known as your voice box, will start to expand, deep down in your throat. You know how a big bass drum sounds compared to a snare drum? Well, as your voice box gets bigger, your voice will become lower and deeper, more like the bass drum.

I'm sure you'll be delighted with your new voice. But the in-between stages aren't so great: Your voice will crack and crackle, and you won't be able to predict when it will be high and when it will be low. One of my son's friends was called on in history class once. The answer to the question was "Trojan War," and he said "Trojan" in a deep voice and "War" in a high, squeaky one. That must have been ten years ago, but when my son and his friends get together, all somebody has to say is "Trojan War" and they all laugh.

A year or so after the voice starts to change, you'll find that hair is beginning to grow under your arms and on your upper lip. In our culture, boys don't shave under their arms. As a matter of fact, I don't think boys shave under their arms in *any* culture. So you've got nothing to worry about there.

But boys *do* shave their faces. (True, some men wear full beards, but not too many junior-high-school kids do.) And when the first "peach fuzz" appears, it's time to start. I know some guys are embarrassed about it. They sneak into the bathroom to use their fathers' razors, or they buy their own and hide them in their rooms. This kind of sneaking around doesn't make any sense—the first shave should be a time to celebrate. It shows that a boy is growing up.

So here's what you do. When your lip starts to get a little fuzzy, announce it in no uncertain terms to your parents. Tell your father that you need a razor, and that you need him to teach you how to use it. If your father isn't around, your mother can teach you just as well.

Believe me, your parents will thank you for breaking the ice. They might even want to make a party out of it, invite relatives, and put the whole thing on videotape.

Your body hair will continue to fill in over the next few years, possibly into your twenties, not only on your face and under your arms, but also on your chest, arms, and legs. As with everything else, there is no "normal" amount of body hair. Some men are almost hairless; some have hair everywhere except their palms and the soles of their feet.

While all of these changes are taking place, plenty is happening inside your body, too. Most important is that your body begins to produce sperm, tiny, tiny cells that try to join a female's ovum after sexual intercourse in order to create a fetus. When you reach puberty, your testes begin to make and store sperm cells by the millions.

The testes keep making more sperm all the time, until there's no room for any more. It has to be released, and it is. It blends with a milky liquid to form *semen,* and the mixture—about a teaspoon's worth—comes out of your penis, from the same opening out of which you urinate. This is called *ejaculation,* and it usually takes place when your penis is erect.

And when does a male ejaculate? A man can ejaculate when he has sexual intercourse, while his penis is inside a woman's vagina. That's how his sperm enter her ovum. Ejaculation usually happens at the same time as *orgasm,* also called *climax,* a very strong, pleasurable feeling, a release of sexual tension, which lasts for a few seconds.

For boys and men, there are two other possibilities for ejaculation. The first is during *masturbation.* To masturbate means to touch or stroke your penis so that it feels good. (Girls masturbate, too, usually by stroking the clitoris or touching the area around or inside the vagina until they have an orgasm.) Many boys masturbate at a young age, without ejaculating. If they do it after puberty, they can ejaculate.

The other possibility, which is probably more common, is that you will ejaculate during sleep, when you have a *nocturnal emission,* sometimes known as a wet dream. (*Nocturnal* means having to do with the nighttime. *Emission* means a sending forth or discharging of something.) You may be having a dream at the time, and the dream may or may not have to do with sex. You may not be aware of dreaming at all. In any case, you usually wake up shortly after the emission, and you find that your sheets or pajamas are moist. Within an hour or so, the wet spots stiffen and leave a slight stain.

Sometime later, if you haven't masturbated or had an ejaculation for any other reason in the meantime, you will probably have another nocturnal emission. And so it will go, for the rest of your life.

A wet dream can be a scary thing, especially the first time it happens. Some boys think they may have wet their beds. Others feel ashamed. This is nonsense. Every boy has wet dreams. Your parents know all about them—especially your father. Any stains the nocturnal emissions leave can easily be washed out. And even if you didn't want to have them, there's absolutely nothing you can do to prevent them.

Unfortunately, a lot of boys don't realize this. One of the boys who was at the children's home with me told me years later, when we were both adults, that whenever he had a wet dream at the age of fourteen, he thought he had peed. Each time, he secretly took his sheets to the laundry room and washed them himself. By the time he was in his twenties, he told me, he had decided he would make certain no son of his ever had the same fears. Sure enough, my friends had a boy, and by the time the boy was ten years old, he was looking *forward* to his first wet dream.

Incidentally, some boys worry about the fact that semen and urine come out of the same place. Can they ever come out at the same time? Do you ever urinate just as you're about to ejaculate? No and no.

When you're about to ejaculate, a special valve outside the bladder, where the urine is stored, closes so that the urine can't get out.

I don't think I'll *ever* get over how amazing the body is.

Boys and Girls: Skin

Everybody sweats, even babies. But when you reach puberty, you'll probably notice that you're perspiring more. This isn't only because teenagers notice *everything* more. It's also because the sweat glands everybody has beneath their skin become more active with puberty, especially under the arms, around the genitals, and on the hands and feet, and especially when a person is nervous or excited.

So what's the problem? Well, you know those deodorant commercials you've been seeing on TV for as long as you can remember? The reason they exist is that when sweat stays under the arms for a long period of time, an odor develops that smells bad to some people. (By the way, this is *another* thing that bothers Americans more than it does people in other countries.)

If you're worried about body odor, here are some things you can do. First, shower or bathe regularly. Second, wear clean, freshly laundered clothes. Third, wear cotton underwear and shirts—cotton absorbs better than synthetic fibers. And finally, if you think you need it, use a deodorant. Buy whichever one smells good to you—they're all pretty much alike.

As the sweat glands are starting to work overtime, so are the oil glands, which are also located just beneath the skin. Your skin and scalp will get oilier, and you may get *acne* on a number of parts of your body. Especially prone to it are the face, the chest, and the back. Acne is a skin condition—usually involving pimples, blackheads, and whiteheads—that occurs when the pores become blocked by a substance the oil glands make, called *sebum*.

Acne is a pain. Not only can it hurt, but it can be embarrassing. Unfortunately, eight out of ten teenagers get it to some degree, and if you're one of the eight, there's not much you can do about it.

People used to feel that certain foods—chocolate, shellfish, fried foods—helped bring on acne, but today doctors aren't sure. They *are* sure that it's not caused by masturbation. And they know that washing regularly helps clear away the oils that contribute to acne.

It probably won't be much comfort at the time, but try to remember that acne is only a passing phase: By the time most people reach their mid to late teens, it's cleared up.

If you have a bad case of acne, you might want to see a *dermatologist,* a doctor who specializes in disorders of the skin. He or she can prescribe some medicines that might help. *Tetracycline,* for example, can fight the infections that often start in clogged pores and can stop the oil glands from making too much sebum. The doctor might also prescribe a cream with *retinoic acid,* which can do a great job of clearing up facial acne.

2

Your Feelings

When my daughter was ten or eleven years old, she and I had a huge fight. I don't really remember what it was about—I think she may have wanted to buy a certain dress, and I thought it wasn't appropriate for a ten-year-old. Anyway, doors were slammed and voices were raised all over the place. That night I was talking on the phone with a friend of mine and I said, "I guess she's at the 'difficult' age."

My friend said, "Ruth, from now on, they're *all* difficult ages."

She had a point.

At around eight or nine, kids start the slow process of becoming grown-ups. It's *never* easy to make that big a change, and along the way there are bound to be a lot of rough times, times when you're angry or sad, times when you don't like anyone, including yourself. Maybe it will help you to realize that you're not the only one who feels this way.

Friends

Do you have a best friend? Somebody you spend hours and hours with, tell everything to, share secrets and private jokes with? If you do, you're lucky. You should also know that not all friendships last. When kids start approaching their teenage years, they begin to develop all

kinds of new interests. Sometimes they even seem to develop a new personality. And suddenly they don't have that much in common with the person who used to be almost like their twin.

I have a younger friend, Debbie, who's now in her thirties. When she was growing up, a girl named Barbara lived around the corner from her. As soon as they were out of diapers, they did everything together. They made up stories about witches and fairies in a nearby forest, they joined the Girl Scouts and giggled about the troop leader, they made up their own private names for each other.

Then, all of a sudden, at the age of fourteen, Debbie got *very* interested in boys. She always wanted to put on makeup and go to the mall, where a lot of cute guys liked to hang out. That didn't seem like much fun to Barbara. *She'd* gotten interested in school, and she preferred to stay home and read a good book. There were other girls who liked to go to the mall, and there were other girls who liked to read, so Barbara and Debbie each made a new group of friends.

When they saw each other in the halls at junior high school and high school, they nodded and smiled, and sometimes chatted a little

bit, but the old closeness was gone. They each had moved on to new stages of their lives.

But I've got to tell you the end of the story. Over the last few years, Barbara and Debbie have gotten close again. They both have children of their own now, and Debbie—who moved away to another city after she finished college—makes sure to visit Barbara and her family every year when she visits her hometown. Debbie even asked Barbara to be the godmother of her one-year-old daughter.

By the way, this kind of thing is even more likely to happen if your best friend is a member of the opposite sex. When kids are really young, boys are friends with girls, and girls are friends with boys, and nobody seems to care. But there comes a point when *everybody* seems to understand that this has to change. I remember when my son was nine. He had always played with girls, but all of a sudden he didn't want to be seen with them. When we were out walking one day, he insisted that we cross to the other side of the street because he saw a girl he knew coming toward us.

And woe to the brave boy who likes to play with dolls with the girls, or to the girl who shoots baskets with the guys! People will say the boy's a "sissy," and the girl's a "tomboy."

One reason kids call other kids names like this may be that they're jealous. They've started to get very interested in the opposite sex, but they're afraid to do anything about it, so they stay with their own kind. If you're the one who's being called tomboy or sissy, just remember that the kids doing the name-calling probably would *love* to be in your shoes.

At about the age of eleven or twelve, boys and girls start going around in groups together. There are parties, and bull sessions, and impromptu get-togethers at community centers, street corners, or malls. This is the best way to ease into dating and the more serious relationships that will come later.

But groups have their own perils. Sometimes *cliques* form, small groups of kids who seem to think that nobody in the world exists except them. If there's a clique in your school that you'd love to be in, but doesn't seem to want you, my advice would be to forget it. There's bound to be another group of kids who'll appreciate you. You'll find that being with them is a lot more fun than moping about not being in a particular clique.

Another problem that results from kids getting together in groups is rumors. When I was at the children's home in Switzerland, I had a boyfriend named Walter. One day I found out that the kids were saying that I had taken all my clothes off for him. This wasn't true, and I was very upset. The worst thing was that the more I denied it, the more everybody seemed to believe it.

I finally decided to ignore the rumor. And do you know what? That was when I stopped hearing it. So remember to ignore kids who tease and spread rumors. It works!

Groups are also responsible for what we call *peer pressure.* You've probably heard this expression, since grown-ups seem to blame it for everything kids do wrong. The fact is, when everyone in your group is urging you to do something that, deep down, you really don't want to do, when they're saying that you're a chicken if you don't do it, it's *hard* to say no. Everybody wants to be accepted, and it sometimes seems that the only course is to go along with the group.

All I can say about responding to peer pressure is that you should *try* to listen to your own conscience, especially when you're being pressed to do things that can be very harmful to you, like drinking or taking drugs. It might help if you talked to someone about it. If you don't think your parents would understand, try an older brother or sister, or maybe an uncle or aunt.

While I'm talking about friendship, I *have* to say a word about the telephone. It's so much a part of kids' lives these days that I don't see how we could have had friendships back when I was young. When my daughter was twelve, it seemed to me that she spent every waking minute on the phone. If she could have talked on the phone in her sleep, she would have done that, too.

What if someone had been calling us with some important news? The person wouldn't have been able to get through because my daughter was on the line. But she refused to get off. Often we had real fights. Finally, I came up with a solution. For my daughter's thirteenth birthday, we gave her her own telephone line. All of a sudden, we were one big happy family again.

Now, your parents may not be able to buy you your own line. For considerably less money, today they can get "call waiting" (it wasn't available when my daughter was a teenager), which at least allows a caller to get through and leave a message. In any event, try to explain to your parents that you need to talk to your friends—and try to understand that sometimes your parents need to talk to *theirs*.

Moods

When you were a very little kid, you didn't really have moods. Sure, you could be miserable and cry your eyes out, but if you got a new toy five minutes later, you probably forgot all about what was upsetting you.

As you got older, your feelings—what we call *emotions*—got stronger. Now you might be down in the dumps for days at a time, or you might feel happier than you've ever been before. You won't always think so, but this is one of the neat things about growing up. Even adults don't feel things as intensely as teenagers, and a lot of them wish they did. I know I think fondly of the days when everything that happened seemed so important.

Of course, it isn't easy to deal with the bad feelings—jealousy, insecurity, anger, or just plain sadness. But it always helps to talk about them, either to a friend or to an adult you can trust.

Some things you'll feel you can't talk about to *anybody*. That's where diaries come in. I'm all for a diary, a special, secret book all your own, where you can write anything that's on your mind. I started keeping one when I first went to the children's home, at the age of ten, and I still have it.

When I read it today, I'm amazed at how miserable I sometimes was. For example, one day when I was thirteen, I wrote, "I am ugly, I am stupid. What will become of me? What right do I have to be alive? . . . I am a hollow, empty, superficial thing."

I must have thought it was the end of the world. But then, a couple of pages later, after I had started to see Walter, I copied this quotation from a sentimental book I'd been reading: "How beautiful it was. Can something be a sin if it was so wonderful? We kissed for the first time, and then both did not know how it happened. It was a wonderful secret and will remain that way for a lifetime."

So remember: No bad feeling lasts forever.

But sometimes bad feelings last longer, and are more painful, than kids think they can bear. Sometimes it may seem that life just isn't worth living anymore. If you ever feel that way, I would strongly advise you to talk to someone whose job it is to help people with their problems. He or she might be called a therapist, a psychologist, a social worker, or a counselor. Your mother, your father, someone else you trust in the family, your teacher, or a school guidance counselor could help you find one. If you don't feel you can talk to them about it, you can even look for one under "psychologist" in the yellow pages of the phone book.

While I'm talking about feelings, I have to say something about what might be the worst one for a kid: embarrassment. As you get older, you find that you get embarrassed a lot more easily. If you

make a mistake or say something that you think is stupid, or if someone makes fun of you, or if one of your parents says almost *anything* in front of your friends, you might feel yourself blushing and find that you won't know what to say.

I'm sorry to say it, but there's no way to avoid embarrassment. Just remember: Kids sometimes feel that *everybody* is looking at them or thinking about them, and that's why they get embarrassed. But it isn't true. Most of the time, people are worried about their *own* problems and haven't even noticed whatever it is you've done.

As I said before, no one *feels* things as strongly as teenagers do. The older teens get, the less often they think the world is going to end. Remembering this might give you a little bit of comfort as you face your latest crisis.

Privacy

Is it important to you to have someplace to go where you're absolutely alone, and no one can bother you or see what you're doing? If not, it probably will be before long. If you're a girl who always used to take baths with your little brother, suddenly you might not want to anymore. If you never used to like to be by yourself in your room, now there will be times when you can't stand the thought of being with anyone else. This need for privacy is something that most teenagers and grown-ups have.

There are lots of things that kids need privacy to do. Like practicing the latest dance steps in front of the mirror, for example. Or writing in a diary. Or talking on the phone with a friend. Or maybe just lying down and thinking.

If you have your own room, make sure your parents understand that it's *your* room. When the door is closed, they should knock before coming in. Some moms and dads might have a hard time understanding this. To drive the point home, make a Do Not Disturb sign out of cardboard and string and hang it on the outside doorknob.

If you share a room with a brother or sister, you might have to go to the bathroom and lock the door to get privacy. Or you could fix up a space in the basement or attic and go there whenever you want to be by yourself.

Self-Image

As kids approach the age of puberty, they often start to think a lot about their bodies. They think about how much they've changed, and how great their bodies have become.

But sometimes they also think that their bodies aren't so great. When I was at the children's home, I thought of myself as short and ugly. I was miserable because I knew I would never look like Shirley Temple, a young movie star who was almost exactly my age and had been acting since she was a little girl.

If only I knew then what I know now—that I looked just fine! I *should* have known it—Walter liked me, and he was a smart boy. But I was convinced that I was unattractive, and it took me many years to learn otherwise.

Here's my advice to you: When you're all alone in your room, take a good long look at yourself in the mirror. You can even take off all your clothes if you want. Smile. Give the mirror your handsomest, prettiest, sexiest look. Then just decide to like what you see. Next, focus on what you think is your best feature—maybe it's your nose. Tell yourself, "What a cute nose I have!" Now, this may sound silly to you, but I think you'll be surprised to find how powerful positive thinking really is.

A lot of kids—girls, especially—think they're too fat. The chances

are you're not too fat at all. But if you really want to lose weight, ask your parents to set up an appointment with a doctor who can tell you the best way to do it. Girls who think much, much too much about losing weight sometimes get so upset that they never want to eat anything at all. This is called *anorexia*. Or they might eat, then make themselves throw up. This is called *bulimia*. Both behaviors are very dangerous and unhealthy. If you ever find yourself acting either way, please talk about it with an adult you trust.

When boys reach puberty, they're often delighted that they can develop muscles. They lift weights and work out, and have a great time walking around with their shirts off. If this is what you like to do, I say, enjoy!

In trying to find out how they can look their best, kids do a lot of experimenting with their hair and their clothes. This is a normal and healthy part of growing up, but let me give you a tip: If you do anything that can't be undone, or can't be undone for a long time, you might regret it.

Even the wildest punk haircut with the most gooey goo in it can look nearly ordinary after a good shampoo and a good combing out. But if you dye your hair purple, you'll be stuck with purple hair for months. It would be better to use a hair coloring that can be washed right out. And I strongly advise you not to do anything permanent, like get a tattoo or have your nose pierced. It might seem like fun at the time, but I bet you'll be sorry in the morning.

Clothes are *very, very* important to a lot of kids your age. You feel you have to have just the right sneakers and just the right sweater, no matter how much they cost. I know this because I see it. But I have a hard time understanding it, because in the children's home every-one wore the same thing: a uniform.

As a matter of fact, I'm in favor of kids wearing uniforms to school. It would eliminate a lot of silly competition, and it would save parents a lot of money.

But a kid's wardrobe is a matter to be decided between the kid and his or her parents. If you can convince your parents to buy you what you want, or if you want to spend your own money on it, good for you.

Parents

I'd be willing to bet that you had at least one fight with your parents in the last week. If not, you're probably due for one tonight!

I'm kidding about this, but it's true that as boys and girls approach their teenage years, there's often a lot of tension between them and their parents. It's only natural: Kids are changing so fast that their parents don't always know how to react to them.

The causes of this tension are usually the following: The parent doesn't like the child's clothing, hairstyle, or makeup. The child wants to stay out later than the parent wants, or go out with certain people or to a certain place the parent doesn't consider safe or appropriate. The parent thinks the child's room is too messy. The child is not getting good enough grades to suit the parent. (I know these sources of conflict so well, because I fought about every one of them with my son or daughter.)

With kids trying to establish their individuality and parents being responsible for them, conflicts are unavoidable. But they can be handled badly or well. Kids, I'd like to ask you to do me a favor and try to understand your mother and father's point of view. They really have your best interests at heart—even if it sometimes doesn't seem that way.

And here's an important tip: Instead of lying to your parents, try to face the conflict head on. Lying can only lead to trouble in the long run. Most of the time, you'll be found out, anyway, and eventually your parents simply won't trust you.

Of course, your parents should try to understand *you*. In fact, I'm going to say something on behalf of kids, and if you want your parents to hear it, now's the time to call them.

Parents: Give your kids a break. They can't always be the obedient, polite, neat, quiet, thrifty, perfect little children you'd like them to be. Please, respect their privacy and their judgment, and try to appreciate them for the people they are.

3

Sex and Other Kinds of Love

Sexuality affects us differently at different ages. It's not that important for little kids. True, boys will find that it feels good to touch the penis, and girls will find that it feels good to touch the area around the vagina, especially the clitoris. But this usually isn't a very big part of their lives.

Love is always a big part of our lives. That's because it has so many different meanings. After all, you can love your mother, and your best friend, and chocolate ice cream, and playing baseball. And as you approach your teens, you probably will begin to love members of the opposite sex.

Crushes

The first time that kids start to have strong feelings about members of the opposite sex is usually about the age of ten or eleven. Up until then, boys (if you're a girl) or girls (if you're a boy) always seemed yucky. But then, all of a sudden, there's one particular boy or girl who seems *fascinating*. The strong feeling you have for this person is called a *crush*.

I remember my first crush. I had it when I was ten and still lived in Frankfurt. A boy named Justin, who was two years older than I, lived above us. I remember thinking how wonderful that was—if anybody picked on me, Justin would protect me. I now realize one of the reasons I developed the crush was that I really wanted an older brother.

You might know the person you have a crush on, or he or she might be someone you just see across a crowded classroom. The object of your crush might be someone older, a brother or sister's friend, a friend of your parents, or maybe a teacher. This person might even be a movie star or a singer. It could be someone of the

opposite sex, or of the same sex. It's perfectly normal to enjoy think-ing this way about people, and sometimes it even turns out that the person you have a crush on has a crush on you! Crushes usually go away in a month or two, and sometimes even less than that.

The Next Step

A year or two later, boys and girls start to spend time together. There are boy-girl parties, where there might be kissing games like spin the bottle. I'm sure kids today play doctor, the way we used to at the children's home. We didn't need to touch each other's private parts—it was fun to touch each other anywhere! I still remember playing tag. How great it was to be "it" and get to hug all the boys.

But if these things don't appeal to you, or you're just not ready for them, you don't have to do them. If you don't feel comfortable about just leaving, I give you permission to tell a white lie—that your mother needs you to go shopping or you have a doctor's appoint-ment. Don't forget—you are in control.

Before long, boys and girls will start to date, and then one brave pair of kids will be the first to call each other boyfriend and girl-friend. They'll hold hands in the hallway at school, look into each other's eyes, and say they'll love each other forever. But the relation-ship usually doesn't last that long.

My first boyfriend actually wasn't Walter. He was a boy at the home, named Max. When I was thirteen, I started helping him with his homework, and I soon developed a big crush on him. "I've come to like Max very much," I wrote in my diary. Then I added a note to myself: "But you've got to pull yourself together."

Soon Max and I were playing doctor together, and I was in heaven. Then tragedy struck: I caught Max kissing another girl. Luckily, Walter was on the horizon, and we started seeing each other.

We had a great time. When we went to class, I sometimes brought a big coat to put on my lap. Underneath it, we used to hold hands. We'd meet under the stairway, or in caves in the woods near the school, and hug and kiss. Walter lived upstairs from me, and he figured out a way to send notes back and forth through the window with little pieces of paper and two strings. We didn't have money to buy each other things, but he made me a wonderful present—a little heart made out of two pieces of leather, one side red, the other side blue. I wore it pinned to my clothes all day, and when I went to sleep at night I pinned it to my pajamas.

My husband's name is Fred, not Walter, so you know that *that* romance didn't last forever, either. We were together for about three years, but then I got jealous because Walter was paying a lot of attention to an older woman, somebody who worked at the home. He assured me that he liked me better, but the end was near. Believe it or not, the final breakup came after a fight we had about something that seemed incredibly important at the time. I wanted him to comb his hair straight back, and he wanted to comb it sideways. As I wrote in my diary, "Enough. That's it. It's over."

My relationship with Walter was very, very important to me. And the best thing about it is that we're still friends today!

Masturbation

When you reach puberty, you'll probably find yourself spending a lot of time thinking about things you're not used to thinking about. Things like kissing or being touched by a boy or girl you know, a movie star, or even a pretty or handsome teacher. When kids have thoughts like that, they might get sexually *aroused*. They start to breathe hard; their faces get flushed. Boys have erections, and girls find that the area inside the vagina becomes moist. What they're feeling is the *sex drive*, an incredibly important part of every human being's makeup.

Boys and girls who've started to have these feelings sometimes masturbate. As I said before, even little kids masturbate by touching their genitals to feel good. But after puberty begins, the urge to do it will probably become stronger and more frequent.

A boy usually masturbates by making a fist around the penis and rubbing up and down. After a while—it could be a few seconds or it could be a few minutes—he will have an orgasm. At the same time, he will ejaculate. The first time a boy does this, it can be quite a shock to see the semen coming out of the penis. The next time, he'll be sure to have a tissue ready to absorb it. Or he might masturbate in the shower.

After a boy ejaculates, his body needs some time to rest, and he probably won't be able to have another erection and ejaculate again for a little while. He probably won't want to, either.

As I said before, a girl masturbates by rubbing the clitoris or the area around or inside the vagina with her fingers. If she keeps doing it, she will have an orgasm. Girls don't ejaculate when they have an orgasm, but by that point they feel very moist from the vaginal secretions that sexual arousal causes.

Sometimes boys like to look at sexy pictures in magazines when they masturbate. (For some reason, this kind of thing doesn't usually seem to interest girls as much.) If you have such magazines, make sure your parents understand that they're your private, personal property.

There's absolutely nothing wrong with masturbating. Most people do it, and it doesn't have any bad effects. There used to be a lot of stories about it—you may have heard some of them—but none are true. It doesn't make you blind or retarded, it doesn't make boys run out of semen, and it won't affect your sex life when you get older. And

masturbation will *never* make girls get pregnant or boys or girls get sexually transmitted diseases. Most important of all, it doesn't make you a bad person.

There's also nothing wrong with *not* masturbating. Some people aren't interested in it, and that doesn't make them any less sexy.

One thing to remember, though, is that masturbation should be done in private. Close your door if you do it in your room, and make it clear to your family that they're not to walk into your room without knocking. If you're afraid they'll barge in, you can put a piece of heavy furniture in front of the door.

Sometimes groups of boys will masturbate together. There's nothing wrong with doing this in privacy.

Homosexuality

Again, *homosexuals* are people who are sexually attracted to people of their own sex. In other words, they're men who are attracted to men and women who are attracted to women. Sometimes homosexuals are called *gay* people. (*Heterosexuals*—men who are attracted to women and women who are attracted to men—are sometimes called *straight*.) Some people are *bisexuals*. That is, they're attracted to people of both sexes.

A long time ago, there was a lot of prejudice against homosexuals. Much prejudice still exists, and some gays feel that they have to keep their sexual preference a secret. But more and more people now understand that homosexuals are healthy and normal and, except for their sexual preference, exactly like everybody else.

Are you homosexual? It's difficult to know. Some people don't figure out if they're gay or straight until their late teens or their twenties. Having a crush on, or even kissing or touching, someone of your own sex does not necessarily mean that you're gay.

Getting Physical

What is sexy behavior? Looking into the eyes of someone you really like is *very* sexy. So are holding hands, walking arm in arm, kissing, and hugging. These are things that almost every young couple does.

Again, privacy is very important. And finding it can be hard, especially if you're too young to drive or you don't have a car. But American kids are geniuses when it comes to finding places to be alone, so I don't think you need my advice on this score.

When boys and girls get older, and get to know each other better, they may want to "go further." Maybe they will *pet*—in other words, touch each other in the places that are most pleasurable to them.

Whether or when to do these things is something every person has to decide for him or herself. But here is something I am very certain and feel very strongly about. You should *not* do anything unless you're sure you're ready to do it, you want to do it, and you feel good about doing it.

Sometimes people will try to pressure you into doing these things. Maybe your boyfriend will say, "If you really loved me, you would do it." Or, if you're a boy, maybe your friends will brag about all the things they've done and act as if you're not a real "man" if you haven't done them, too.

This is nonsense. If your boyfriend feeds you a line like that, he really doesn't love you. Or respect you. And kids who brag about all the things they've done usually aren't even telling the truth.

Sometimes a girl will do things she doesn't want to do because she

thinks it will make her be liked. This is an understandable way to feel, but it doesn't really make sense. It's like a rich boy trying to "buy" friends by giving them presents or money. They don't like him. They just like what they're getting, and when the presents stop, they won't be his friends anymore.

Sexual Intercourse

In sexual intercourse, a man and a woman lie down together. After they hug and kiss and stroke and maybe talk to each other for a little while (or a long time), the man inserts his erect penis into the woman's vagina. Because the vagina creates its own moisture when a woman is sexually aroused, the penis goes in easily. Then the man and woman each move their hips so that the penis will slide in and out. Usually the man will reach orgasm and ejaculate as a result of intercourse, and the woman may have an orgasm.

After sex, when the man has taken his penis out, a couple should have a nice warm feeling. They might hold each other and give each other tender kisses. If the woman has not had an orgasm, the man might stroke her clitoris until she has one. After a while, they may be ready to have sex again. Or they may not.

How often do people have sex? Well, some husbands and wives do it every day. Other couples do it once a week, once a month, or maybe less often than that. Couples find that at different stages of their lives, they're more or less interested in sex. But many people are very active sexually as long as they live.

The first time a female has sexual intercourse, the penis may stretch her hymen—the thin layer of skin that partially blocks the vaginal opening—and sometimes a little blood may come out. But not always—and if there is no blood, it *doesn't* mean that a girl has had sex before.

When kids hear about sexual intercourse for the first time, they sometimes think it sounds strange, or even disgusting. That's a natural reaction. Sex only makes sense when it's connected to feelings for another person. Kids don't have these feelings yet, and won't really understand them until they do.

Kids also sometimes think that when a man's penis is inside a woman's body, he might urinate. This can't happen. As I told you before, there's a special valve outside the bladder that closes when a male is about to ejaculate.

Another scary thing about sexual intercourse is that when a man and woman do it, they may make a lot of noise—shouts and screams and grunts and all kinds of sounds. A girl I knew in the children's home told me she once heard her parents when they were having sex, and she was very frightened because she thought her father was beating up her mother. Well, for a lot of people, making noise makes sex more fun.

By the way, if you ever walk into your parents' room and find that they're having sex, you should act the same way you wish *they* would act if they came into your room and found you doing something private. Just say, "Excuse me," and walk right out again. You might want to talk about it with them later. They might want to talk about it with you. Or both of you might feel more comfortable not talking about it at all.

Sexual intercourse is sometimes called "going all the way," and with good reason. Deciding to do it is a very serious thing, for at least three reasons. First, sexual intercourse can lead to pregnancy. Having a baby is something that will change anyone's life forever and that not many people are ready for until they're at least in their twenties and married.

Second, it can lead to illness, the contracting of any sexually transmitted disease, including the most dangerous one, AIDS.

And finally, sexual intercourse can lead to disappointment, even unhappiness, if it's not warm, loving, and joyous, shared by two people who feel strongly about each other and know exactly what they're doing. That's why it's sometimes called "making love." It's such a powerful experience that no teenagers I know are ready for it.

So let me repeat what I said before about people who try to convince you to have sex. Try as *hard* as you can not to let them influence you. There are good reasons to have sex. But there are also very bad reasons, like trying to be popular, or being pressured by your boyfriend or girlfriend, or trying to get back at your parents, or trying to prove that you're grown up, or wanting to do what everybody else does.

People who have not yet had sexual intercourse are called *virgins*. If you watch certain TV shows or listen to certain records or go to certain R-rated movies, you might think that *nobody* past a certain age is a virgin. That's not true at all. A lot of people are virgins until they get married. Some people, including Catholic priests and nuns, are virgins their whole lives. I'll tell you one thing for sure: People who are not virgins always remember where and when and to whom they lost their virginity.

4

Contraception

Sexual intercourse is usually necessary to start the process that ends with a baby being born. But men and women have sexual intercourse for reasons besides having children. The main one is that when they love each other, sex can be a warm and very pleasurable experience.

That's fine. But people who have sex have to remember something: With very few exceptions, any time a man and a woman have sexual intercourse, there's a chance that the woman will become pregnant.

For some couples, having a baby wouldn't be a good idea. This is especially true of young people. A fifteen-year-old boy and girl are biologically able to become parents. But they would be completely unprepared to take on the incredible responsibility that comes with being a parent.

This is true of older kids, too. Let's say a boyfriend and girlfriend are about to graduate from high school. They have all sorts of plans. She wants to go on to college, then law school, and one day become a judge. He wants to learn to be an architect. If they have a baby, almost all of the time, money, and love they have will have to be devoted to the baby. This doesn't leave much room for their dreams.

It doesn't leave them much *time* to dream, either. A baby means no full night's sleep for a long time; no movies; no peaceful, uninterrupted meals; little time even to talk to each other. If a couple doesn't have a solid relationship, they'll know it within a few weeks after a baby is born.

Some girls might think they *want* to get pregnant. Imagine a girl who's a little lonely. Maybe her self-image isn't very good. She's always liked cuddling dolls, and she's even baby-sat her one-year-old niece. She thinks that having a real live baby of her own, a baby that she could love and that would love *her,* would be wonderful.

But babies aren't like dolls. They aren't like nieces, either, because they're around all the time. They need almost constant love and attention.

If a couple is sure they want to have sex, but don't want to have a baby, they must use *contraception,* or birth control. There are many different kinds of contraception, but they all try to prevent the man's sperm and the woman's ovum from coming together during intercourse and becoming implanted in the uterine wall. Some of the methods work very well. And some of them don't work at all.

First I'll tell you about the ones that don't work at all. Some people think that if a couple has sex standing up, the woman can't get pregnant. Wrong.

Or if a woman is having sex for the first time, she can't get pregnant. Wrong.

Or if a woman *douches,* or washes out her vagina with a certain kind of liquid, immediately after sex, she can't get pregnant. Wrong.

Or if she doesn't have an orgasm, she can't get pregnant. Wrong.

Or if she urinates right after sex, she can't get pregnant. Wrong.

Many couples try to avoid pregnancy by *withdrawal.* This means that, just before he ejaculates, the man will take his penis out of the woman's vagina. There are two problems with this method. The first is that no male can be completely sure when he's about to ejaculate, and he may be too late. The second is that, even before he ejaculates, some semen oozes out of his penis, putting into the vagina live sperm that can fertilize an ovum.

The *rhythm method* isn't very much more effective. This is also called "natural birth control," and it's the attempt by some couples to figure out exactly when it is "safe" to have sex; that is, when the woman is at the point in her menstrual cycle at which she cannot get pregnant. This is very tricky to do, and should only be tried with the help of doctors or other trained professionals. Even when it's done correctly, it fails a good amount of the time.

Some kinds of birth control work better. But they all have their advantages and disadvantages. And remember: The only absolutely foolproof contraception method is for a man never to put his penis inside a woman's vagina. He shouldn't even put it next to the vagina, because sperm can enter the vagina and swim up to the fallopian tube.

Condoms

Condoms are shaped like the finger of a glove. They're usually made of stretchable rubber, and they can be bought at any drugstore.

Condoms come from the package rolled, so they look a little like small Frisbees. Before sexual intercourse, the man unrolls the condom onto his erect penis, leaving some space at the end. When he ejaculates, his semen stays in the condom and doesn't enter the woman's vagina.

Condoms have no bad side effects, aren't expensive, and are pretty effective birth control. Also, they offer good protection against sexually transmitted diseases. Sometimes, however, they fail by slipping off or breaking.

In Planned Parenthood clinics and in some schools, condoms are distributed free of charge. Some people are against this. They think it

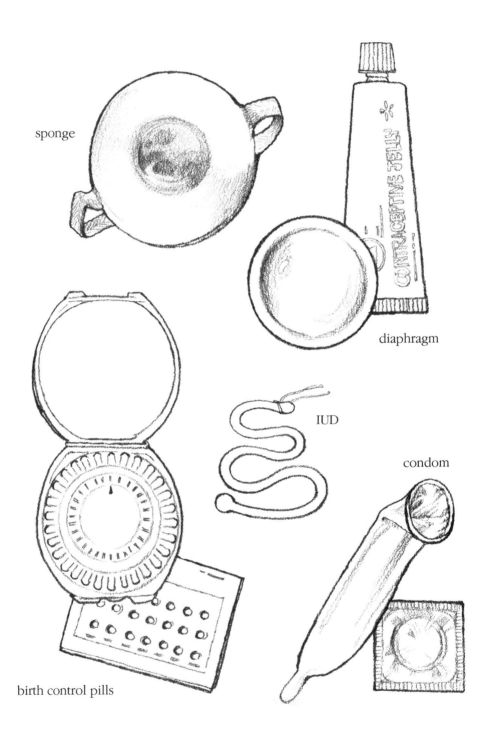

sponge

CONTRACEPTIVE JELLY

diaphragm

birth control pills

IUD

condom

encourages young people to have sex. I disagree. No matter what adults say, *some* young people will have sex. And if they do, it's absolutely necessary that they have contraception.

Unlike most other kinds of birth control, condoms are the male's responsibility. But sometimes boys and men aren't that responsible. They might think it's not "cool" to use a condom, or they might just be embarrassed to walk into a drugstore and buy a package. After all, they might think, *they're* not going to get pregnant. *They're* not going to have to give birth to a baby and be responsible for its well-being.

Any girl or woman whose boyfriend or husband behaves this way owes it to herself to sit him down and give him a good talking-to. And if he doesn't get the point, she owes it to herself to ask herself a question: Is this guy really worth it? Of course, he simply might have forgotten. And since this can happen to anyone, it's a good idea for *her* to carry condoms.

Recently, the Food and Drug Administration gave conditional approval to a female condom, a loose tube that a woman inserts into her vagina before intercourse. No one knows yet just how effective it is, but if it does work well, it will be a welcome addition to the list of birth control methods.

Contraceptive Foams, Jellies, and Creams

Certain substances are *spermicidal*—that is, when they come into contact with sperm, they cause the sperm to die. One kind of contraceptive consists of spermicidal foams, jellies, and creams. The woman inserts one of these substances into her vagina before sex, and if it works, none of the sperm cells will make it into the fallopian tubes.

There are a couple of things to bear in mind about these products (which are available at the drugstore). First, it's very important that anyone using them follow the directions carefully. For example, some people put them in *after* having sex. By then, it's too late.

Second, used alone (even if used properly), the foams, jellies, and creams have a high failure rate. It's much better to use them *with* a condom or diaphragm.

The Diaphragm

A diaphragm is a nearly flat rubber cup made to fit snugly over a woman's *cervix,* the opening that connects her vagina to her uterus. Since the fit is important, it has to be prescribed by a doctor, who shows the woman the right way to put it in place.

Before having sex, the woman places a small amount of spermi-cidal jelly or cream on the diaphragm, and then inserts it. She should keep it in for at least six hours after intercourse, to make sure all the sperm are dead.

Used properly, the diaphragm can be an effective form of contra-ception.

The Pill

When a woman takes birth control pills, she stops ovulating. There-fore, there is no ovum to be fertilized by the man's sperm.

A doctor has to prescribe birth control pills. (It could be danger-ous to take a pill that was prescribed for somebody else.) Starting either the fifth day or the first Sunday after a menstrual period has begun, a woman takes one pill a day for three weeks. Then she stops taking them for a week. Then she starts again.

If used properly, the pill is a very effective form of birth control. However, taking it for just one or two days, or swallowing a bunch of a friend's pills, won't work. And if a woman stops taking the pill, she can get pregnant right away.

Birth control pills are relatively expensive (although they are sold at Planned Parenthood clinics at a discount). They also have some side effects, and women who are thinking about using the pill should discuss them with their doctors.

The IUD

The IUD, or intrauterine device, is a small piece of plastic that a doctor inserts into a woman's uterus. It stays there as long as she wants. Somehow—nobody really knows exactly how—it prevents the fertilized ovum from attaching itself to the wall of the uterus. Some women find that the IUD causes abdominal pain or uncomfortably heavy menstrual flow. These women should find another means of contraception. For others, if the IUD is checked by a doctor every now and then to make sure that it's still in place, it is an effective kind of contraception. The IUD is *not* recommended for women who have not had children.

The Sponge

The contraceptive sponge contains sperm-killing chemicals that are gradually released over a period of about twenty-four hours. A woman inserts it into her vagina, up against the cervix, before intercourse, leaves it there for from six to twenty-four hours afterward, then takes it out and throws it away. It is not a very effective means of contraception.

Sterilization

Another birth control method is *sterilization*—an operation that is performed in a doctor's office or a hospital. Both men and women can be sterilized. In a *vasectomy,* the *vas deferens,* the tube through which the sperm pass, is tied or cut. A man who has had a vasectomy can no longer get a woman pregnant.

There are several different types of female sterilization. All involve blocking the fallopian tubes so that sperm and egg cannot meet.

The main drawback to sterilization is that for women, it's usually permanent. (Men are sometimes able to have their vasectomies reversed.) A woman may think that she never wants to have children, but in ten years may feel differently. If she's been sterilized, she probably won't be able to do anything about it.

Other Contraceptives

There are other contraceptives in use even now, but these have not yet withstood the test of time. I hope that they will be proven safe and effective.

When Contraception Fails

What if contraception fails and a woman who doesn't want to become pregnant gets pregnant? What if a couple doesn't use contraception at all, conceives, and has no desire to have a baby or no ability to raise one? Well, the woman can have the baby, anyway, and have it offered for adoption.

Some babies are taken into loving homes, where foster or adoptive parents raise them as their own children. But the natural mothers must understand that they may not see the children or hear about them again. And other babies are not so lucky. They end up in institutions, or with mothers and fathers who don't treat them well.

If a young girl has a baby, she sometimes decides to keep it and raise it with the help of her own family. Or her parents keep it and raise it as another child of their own. Either arrangement often turns out to be a poor one because of the strains it causes within the family and the burden it places on the girl and her parents.

Marrying the child's father and beginning a home with him is risky, too. This usually is too much for the young parents, and doesn't provide a solid home for the child. Often it results in a *broken* home.

Another option is abortion. This is a medical procedure, performed after a woman becomes pregnant, for removing from the uterus the fertilized egg cell or the embryo it has developed into. Early in the pregnancy, an abortion can be done simply and quickly. Later, the procedure becomes more complicated and the woman needs to stay in the hospital overnight.

Abortion is a *very* sensitive and emotional issue. Some people feel that abortion is murder and should not be allowed. Others feel it should be allowed only under certain circumstances—when the life of the mother is at risk, for example. Others feel it should never be performed after the twelfth week of pregnancy. Others feel it should be available to all women at any time. Currently, different states have different abortion laws and regulations.

I think that abortion should *not* be used as a method of birth control. However, I think that every woman should have the right to choose to have an abortion.

5

Sexually Transmitted Diseases

Although at the right time and under the right circumstances, sex is a happy, healthful experience, sometimes it can make a person sick. This happens when one partner has a sexually transmitted disease.

Sexually transmitted diseases (STDs), some of which are also known as *venereal diseases* (VD), are diseases that are spread through the close contact of two people having sexual intercourse. The main STDs are *gonorrhea, herpes, chlamydia, pubic lice* (also known as crabs), *hepatitis B, syphilis,* and *AIDS*.

STDs are serious for two reasons. First, they can make the person who has them very sick. Second, they make that person a *carrier*. Every time he or she has sex, there is the likelihood that his or her partner will be infected. The likelihood is reduced when the man uses a condom, but it's still there. As with pregnancy, the only absolutely sure way not to catch a sexually transmitted disease is not to have sexual intercourse.

Some signs of sexually transmitted diseases are itching and soreness around the sex organs and a painful sensation while urinating. Except for AIDS, all STDs can be treated medically, and anyone who thinks that he or she might have an STD should immediately see a doctor. If not treated, STDs can cause arthritis, sterility, intense discomfort and pain, blindness, and, in the case of AIDS and syphilis, death.

There is a toll-free number at which counselors will give information about STDs. (They do not ask for the caller's name.) The number in California is 1-800-982-5883. In the rest of the country, it's 1-800-227-8922.

AIDS

AIDS stands for *acquired immune deficiency syndrome*. It is the most serious sexually transmitted disease because it always leads, eventually, to death. The disease, which is caused by a virus called *HIV* (for *human immunodeficiency virus*), damages the body's immune system, its means of fighting *other* kinds of diseases. Because of this, people with AIDS often die from certain kinds of cancer or from pneumonia.

AIDS is also a new disease. The virus was first recognized in 1981. In 1992, over 200,000 people in the United States were known to have AIDS, and many more have it around the world.

People talk about AIDS a lot, and a lot of people aren't well informed about it. The first thing you should know about AIDS is all the ways you *can't* get it. You can't get it from a carrier who sneezes on you, kisses you, hugs you, holds your hand, or touches you in any way, or from one who shares food, cups, or utensils with you. You can't get it from a mosquito bite or from a toilet seat that was used by an AIDS carrier.

How *can* you get AIDS? There are really only three ways. The first is by having sexual intercourse with someone who has AIDS. Although AIDS spread first among homosexual men in this country, heterosexuals do get it and spread it, too.

The second is by having the blood of someone with the virus enter your bloodstream. Many drug users have gotten AIDS by sharing infected hypodermic needles. Some people have gotten AIDS from blood transfusions, but that was before doctors realized that the disease could be spread this way. Today donated blood is tested to make sure that it's safe.

Finally, babies born to a mother with AIDS have a chance of getting the virus.

It's important to remember that people who have AIDS don't always *realize* they have it. They can carry the virus for years without showing any outward signs of the disease. And they are just as infectious before their symptoms are obvious.

As with other sexually transmitted diseases, the only way you can be almost certain not to get AIDS is not to have sexual intercourse. If you are having sexual intercourse, you should have sex with only one partner, someone who has been tested for AIDS and does not have it, and who is having sex only with you. (Keep in mind that AIDS is not detectable until a person has been infected for six months.)

One other way of greatly reducing the risk of getting AIDS is to make sure a condom is always used during sexual intercourse. By the way, some people think they can avoid AIDS by practicing anal intercourse (putting the penis in the anus) or oral sex (putting it in the mouth). They are dead wrong. These practices are just as dangerous as regular intercourse.

While there is still no cure for AIDS, there are some medicines that help to control the damage it does to the body. And scientists are working very hard to develop a *vaccine,* a medicine that will prevent people from getting AIDS. Some people expect that the vaccine will be found within the next ten years.

I hope so.

6

Sexual Abuse

Sex between two people who love each other is one of the greatest joys in life. But there are other kinds of sex that can be very damaging. These result from *sexual abuse*. One form of sexual abuse is called rape, and it involves forcing someone else to have sex. Rape is a crime, and it can happen even when a man and woman, or boy and girl, know each other. (In fact, victims often know their rapists.) If a woman says she does not want to have sex, a man should not force her into it—no ifs, ands, or buts. If he does, that's rape.

Child molestation occurs when grown-ups or teenagers try to get sexually involved with kids, and that's a crime, too. A molester can be a grown-up who touches a child's penis or vagina or tells the child to touch his or hers. He or she can be a grown-up who hugs or kisses a child in a way that isn't right. A molester can be a grown-up who tries to make a child watch sexy movies, or look at sexy pictures, or watch while he or she masturbates. And a molester can be a grown-up who rapes a child by forcing him or her to have sexual intercourse.

If a stranger kisses or hugs you, you know it's wrong. But sometimes you can't really be sure if sexual abuse is happening. Grown-ups who love or like a kid often show their feelings by hugging or kissing. Is anything wrong with that? Probably not. But if it doesn't feel right to you, or if you just don't like it, ask the person to stop as clearly as you can. Your body is private, and you don't have to let anybody touch it. If the person doesn't stop, you can assume that sexual abuse is taking place. Try to get away as quickly as possible. Then, as soon as you can, tell an older person you trust—a parent, a teacher, a guidance counselor, a minister or rabbi, a librarian, or even an older brother or sister—exactly what happened. This is very important. Child molesters often try to convince kids not to tell. They try to make the kid feel ashamed of what happened, that it was somehow his or her fault. They may even say that the kid's parents will get angry at the kid. Sometimes child molesters try to pretend that they "love" the child they abused.

If you are molested, it is *not* your fault. The molester does *not* love you. Even if you later feel that you may have been able to prevent it, you should *not* feel guilty. It's the grown-up's fault, and he or she is the one who should be punished.

How do you avoid situations where you might be sexually abused? Well, as your parents have probably told you a hundred times, don't talk to strangers, especially when they seem to be acting a little too friendly. And if you don't feel right about the way an older person you know is acting toward you, tell a parent or another trusted grown-up about your concerns.

If you *are* molested, remember: *Tell* someone you trust as soon as you can. And *don't* feel guilty.

Incest

You may not think it's possible, but sometimes older kids try to have sex with their younger brothers or sisters, and parents try to have sex with their children. This form of sexual abuse is called *incest*.

I feel very bad for kids who are victims of incest. It is the worst kind of child abuse, because it leaves the kid feeling so confused. He or she loves the parent or sibling, but knows that this person did something very wrong.

And whom can the kid tell about it? The other members of the family might not believe what happened. And the kid might want very much to pretend that it didn't happen, because who wants to be a part of a family in which incest occurs?

The only thing I can say is that, as hard as it is to tell, it's even *worse* not to tell. Having a secret like this is a terrible burden that no one should have to carry. So if you are a victim of incest, admit to yourself what is happening—and tell a trusted adult right away. Keep in mind that you need help, and that the person committing incest needs it, too.

7

How Babies Are Made

Now, I think, is the time to talk about the most important part of the whole subject of sex: the way babies are conceived and born.

Here's how it happens. When a couple has sexual intercourse and the man ejaculates, he sends about 300 million sperm cells into the woman's vagina. Sperm cells are small, really small. If you lined up 500 of them in a row, the row would be just about an inch long.

The only way you can see a sperm cell is through a microscope, where you would see a long tail wagging around. The tail is important. It lets the sperm swim through the cervix, into the uterus, and, after a journey that takes at least an hour, into the fallopian tubes.

Only some of the sperm get that far. Some flow out of the vagina because of gravity. Some die in or are absorbed by the woman's body. But about 2,000 make it to each fallopian tube.

As I said before, about halfway through the menstrual cycle, a woman will ovulate. That is, one of her ovaries will mature and release an egg cell, or ovum. It travels to one of the fallopian tubes, and if it encounters the sperm (coming from the other direction), the sperm will try to get inside the ovum. Sometimes one sperm cell will get in. It will then join with the nucleus of the ovum and *fertilize* it. The woman has conceived—she's officially pregnant.

It's the sperm that determines whether the fertilized ovum will

become a boy baby or a girl baby. There are two types of sperm cells. One carries an X and a Y chromosome, which means the baby will be male; one carries two X chromosomes, meaning it will be female.

Conception does not happen every time a man and a woman have sexual intercourse. The sperm has to get to the fallopian tube as the egg is traveling through it. And even if that happens, the woman will not always get pregnant. Sometimes the sperm just won't get through the egg, and sometimes, for different reasons having to do with their bodies, it may be difficult for the man to fertilize a woman or for the woman to get pregnant.

But remember: Any time a man and a woman have sexual intercourse, it's possible that she will conceive. Trying to figure out just when she's ovulating and then avoiding sex that week is *not* enough to prevent pregnancy. For one thing, it's very hard to know exactly when ovulation happens. For another, sperm cells survive for an average of three days in a woman's body. That makes figuring out when it's "safe" to have sex very, very tricky.

And that's why it's extremely important that if a couple don't want to have a baby, they use contraception, or birth control.

From Embryo to Fetus

After an ovum is fertilized, it continues to travel down the fallopian tube. Five to seven days afterward, it plants itself in the lining of the uterus, where it nourishes itself and grows. It's now called an *embryo*.

Because the embryo needs that lining to survive, the woman does not discard it, and so she doesn't menstruate that month or at any time during her pregnancy.

Missing a period is one of the first signs a woman gets that she might be pregnant. It doesn't tell her anything definite—she could be missing her period for another reason—but if she's recently had sex, she should get a home pregnancy testing kit, which is sold in most drugstores. It's not completely reliable, so if the results indicate pregnancy, the woman should go to a doctor's office, or a Planned Parenthood office or family planning clinic. At any one of these places she can take a test that will let her know for sure. If the results indicate that she is not pregnant and she still hasn't her period a week later, she should try the home test again, just to be sure.

The day that a woman finds out she's pregnant—especially for the first time—is an incredibly important one in her life. I remember the way it was for me. When I heard I was pregnant with my daughter, I was surprised and overjoyed. I'm only four feet, seven inches tall and had always thought that I was too small to have a baby.

By the way, it is safe and completely normal for pregnant women to have sexual intercourse right up until the last stages of pregnancy. If a woman is pregnant, her body stops producing ova until after her baby is born. So even if she has sexual intercourse, she can't get pregnant again. Pregnancy is one of the few surefire methods of contraception I know.

A baby is born a long time after the moment of conception. The period of time between conception and birth is known as the *gesta-*

tion period. In human beings, it averages 266 days, or about eight and a half months. (You might have thought that it was nine months. Nine months is the length of time from the last menstrual period till birth.)

The mother's body provides everything the embryo needs to survive. In her uterus she forms the *placenta,* a flat mass of tissues that surrounds the embryo and passes oxygen and nutrients to it. After about ten weeks, the *umbilical cord* is formed. This is a tube, connected to the embryo's navel, through which nourishment passes.

Every day the embryo grows and develops a little bit more. At four weeks it's about a quarter of an inch long. At eight weeks it's still tiny—about an inch—but it's starting to look like a baby. Now it's called a *fetus,* and it has eyes, ears, arms, hands, fingers, legs, feet, and

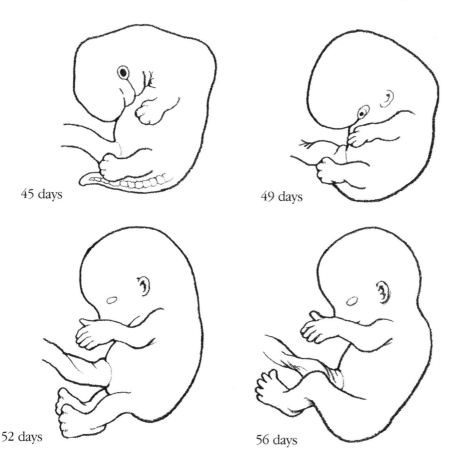

45 days

49 days

52 days

56 days

toes, as well as the beginnings of all its internal organs. By the twelfth week it's four inches long and almost fully developed—it looks like a tiny human being. From then on, it just gets bigger and becomes prepared to live in the world.

Soon after the fourth month of pregnancy, some couples decide to have medical tests done to see how the fetus is doing. The most common test is called *amniocentesis,* and it can reveal whether the baby will be born with certain *birth defects,* such as Down's syndrome, which is a form of mental retardation, and muscular dystrophy. Sometimes, if the fetus is very sick, the parents may decide to have an abortion.

Amniocentesis also shows whether the baby will be a boy or a girl. Some parents ask their doctors not to tell them—they'd rather be surprised.

Sometimes the woman has a *miscarriage.* This means that, for any one of a number of reasons, the embryo or fetus doesn't survive. Miscarriage usually takes place in the first three months of pregnancy.

While I'm talking about things that don't happen very often, let me tell you about twins. You've probably noticed that there are two different kinds of twins. *Identical* twins look alike; *fraternal* twins don't. During ovulation, a woman can release two ova at the same time. If they're both fertilized, the result will be two embryos and eventually a pair of fraternal twins. Sometimes, when just one ovum is fertilized, it divides into two separate embryos; then a pair of identical twins is born. Out of every ninety or so births, one will be a set of twins.

The fetus is able to move much earlier, but is usually felt by the mother sometime in the fourth month of pregnancy. Over the next few months, it will turn around, kick, and move all over inside the uterus.

I remember the first time I felt this faint flutter of activity and knew for sure that a living creature was inside me. It was thrilling.

What It's Like to Be Pregnant

As I said, the first sign of pregnancy is a missed period. The next, for some women, is morning sickness—which means feeling nauseous in, you guessed it, the morning. (For some women, it lasts the whole day.) When I was pregnant with my daughter, I threw up every morning for three months—but with a smile on my face because I was so happy. Most pregnant women also find that their breasts get a little bigger and feel slightly tender.

Pregnancy is also a very emotional time. There are the natural anxieties—will the baby be healthy? will the mother be able to handle the burden of being totally responsible for the well-being of another human being?—and also mood swings that have to do with all the changes the mother's body is going through. She'll be in despair one day, on cloud nine the next. There's nothing a woman can do to prevent this emotional roller coaster, but she may be better able to cope with it if she knows it's coming.

After the first three months, as the fetus gets bigger and bigger, the woman's belly will, too. She'll have to start wearing special *maternity* clothes—loose, billowy pants, dresses and shirts that let her feel comfortable in her new body. Since I didn't have much money when I was pregnant, I had only two maternity dresses. But I always felt wonderful in them.

By the way, even though people say that a baby is inside a woman's "stomach" or "tummy," that's not true. It's in her *uterus*. So what she eats doesn't touch the baby. But because that food reaches the baby through her bloodstream, it's *very* important for a pregnant woman to eat carefully. She needs more protein, iron, calcium, folic acid, and vitamins A, B, C, D, and E. Her doctor can tell her what kinds of foods will give her these nutrients, and will probably prescribe special vitamin supplements for her.

Pregnant women should *not* take drugs, and they shouldn't drink liquor, wine, or beer, either. Smoking can also harm the fetus, and so can drinking coffee. These restrictions are hard for some women to get used to, but they're very important. No one would give liquor to a small child, so a mother *certainly* shouldn't give it to a completely defenseless fetus.

The last three months of pregnancy can be pretty uncomfortable. A woman is carrying around anywhere from twenty to thirty extra pounds. Sometimes her back hurts. Sometimes she just doesn't feel very good. And she's usually really impatient. She and the father probably have picked out names, furniture, and baby clothes. If only the kid would hurry up and be born!

Giving Birth

And then, finally, the day comes. The mother will feel *contractions* in the muscles of the uterus, a feeling of tightening, signaling that her body is getting ready to give birth. At first the contractions are mild and come every fifteen or thirty minutes. When they become strong and begin to come every five to ten minutes, it's time to go to the hospital. A woman should also at least call the doctor if she feels a gush of warm liquid down her legs. What happened is that her water broke. This refers to the release of the amniotic fluid in which the fetus had been sustained in the uterus.

The process of giving birth to a baby is called *labor* for a very simple reason—it's really hard work. For women having their first child, the average length of labor is between twelve and fifteen hours.

Although the contractions can be painful, women can choose to take medicine that makes them much more comfortable during labor. And many mothers, in the last few months of their pregnancy, practice breathing and relaxing in a special way that makes the process of childbirth easier. It also helps to have a loved one—usually the baby's father—with her in the delivery room to hold her hand, feed her ice chips, and coach her in the relaxation techniques.

During labor, the baby travels out of the uterus and through the vagina. Toward the end of labor, the mother will feel an urge to push, almost as if she were having a bowel movement. This helps, too.

Finally the top of the baby's head becomes visible. At this point, the doctor or midwife (a person trained in delivering babies) sees to it that the baby comes the rest of the way.

You may not think it's possible for a human being, even a tiny baby, to fit through a woman's vagina. But it is. One of the wonders of the human body is that when it has to stretch, it stretches. And then it goes back to its normal size.

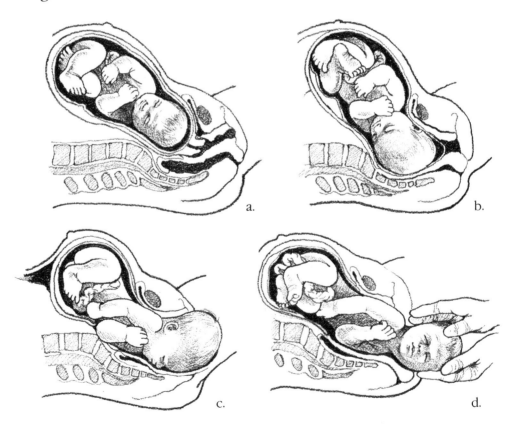

a.

b.

c.

d.

After the baby is born, the doctor, the midwife, or a nurse clears out the baby's mouth, nose, and lungs, and he or she—now the parents *know* if it's a boy or a girl—breathes real air for the first time. Then comes that first cry, which is a sweeter sound than any music I've ever heard. And then the umbilical cord, through which the fetus was connected to the mother, is cut away, leaving a navel, or belly button.

You've probably never seen a baby right after birth. If you have, you know that newborns aren't that great-looking. They're wrinkled, splotchy, and red-faced. Sometimes they're a little misshapen, and they don't have the most intelligent expressions on their faces. But can you blame them? How would *you* look if you'd just been squeezed through a birth canal? Anyway, within a few days, the baby is looking a *lot* better.

Cesareans

Sometimes the doctor helping the mother give birth decides that the normal *vaginal* birth I've just described won't work out. The baby might be in an awkward position. The baby might *need* to get out and be unable to wait until labor has run its course. The baby might really be too big to fit through the birth canal. Or the mother might have a physical condition that makes vaginal delivery inadvisable.

In those cases, the doctor will decide to perform a *cesarean section*. This is a surgical procedure in which the doctor makes an incision through the wall of the abdomen and the uterus, and lifts the baby out. In the United States, about one in five births is performed by cesarean.

The operation is painless because the mother is given medicine. And, although surgery is always a serious matter, it's very safe.

One advantage of cesareans is that since the babies born this way don't have to pass through the birth canal, they usually look much better at birth. Both of my children were born by cesarean sections, and both were beautiful babies.

The First Days of Life

Newborn babies need a lot of help. There's hardly anything they can do for themselves except breathe, urinate, and defecate, and, of course, cry. They can't eat regular food, or even baby food, yet.

One thing they're really good at is sucking, which is fortunate, since all the food they need at birth is in the mother's breasts, theirs for the asking. Amazingly, a newborn baby instinctively seeks out the breast and sucks the mother's milk through her nipple.

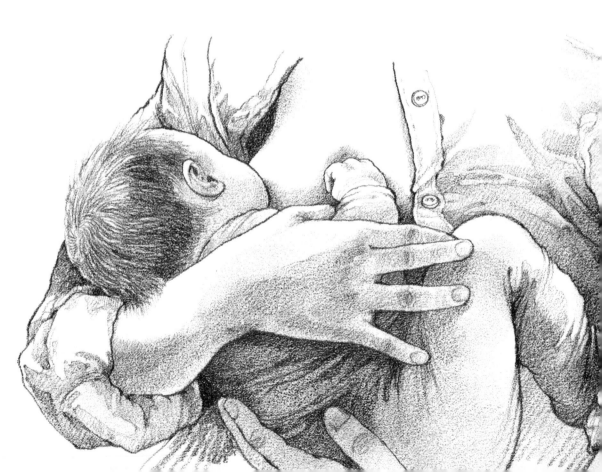

After the child is born, the mother's body will produce breast milk, which has the nutrients the baby needs, as well as substances that prevent disease, and is always just the right temperature—the perfect baby food. The mother will keep producing milk until the baby stops breast-feeding. Breast-feeding is not for everyone, however. Some mothers find it uncomfortable; some have to be away from their babies for long periods at a time (at work or at school); some simply don't like the idea of it. The babies of these mothers are usually fed commercial formula out of a bottle, or a combination of breast milk and formula.

For the first few days, the baby will sleep, wake up, cry, eat, go back to sleep again, and so on. Gradually he or she will get used to being alive, become more alert and responsive, and stay awake for longer periods of time. The baby will want to be cuddled and held a lot. After a little while, he or she will start to develop an individual look and personality.

And then it's only a few short years to puberty!

Afterword

There's a whole new world out there waiting for you: the world of sexuality. It's an exciting world, but it's a little frightening, too.

It probably won't seem so frightening if you take things one step at a time. Enjoy being a kid for as long as you still are a kid, and take time to find pleasure in each new phase of growing up.

I'll stop lecturing you in a minute, but first let me remind you of the three most important things I know about sex. Don't ever feel that you have to do anything you don't want to do. Don't feel guilty about your thoughts or fantasies. And, finally, don't ever try to force someone else into doing anything he or she doesn't want to do.

There are bound to be moments when you will be confused or scared. That's normal. (It would be *ab*normal if there weren't.) During those moments, try to remember that you're not alone: There are people in your life who love you. If you let them in on your feelings, they will gladly try to help you deal with what's bothering you.

Finally, remember that Dr. Ruth believes it is everybody's obligation to try to have a happy life. And a happy life is exactly what I wish for you.

Suggestions for Further Reading

Aho, Jennifer. *Learning about Sexual Abuse.* Enslow, 1985.
   Talks about the different kinds of sexual abuse and how to avoid situations where it might happen.

Gardner-Loulan, JoAnn & Lopez, Bonnie. *Period.* Rev. ed. Volcano Press, 1991.
   Accurate, informative, thorough, positive, and reassuring, this explanation of the biological and emotional aspects of menstruation is practical, down-to-earth, and humorous.

Hyde, Margaret O. & Forsyth, Elizabeth. *Know about AIDS.* Rev. ed. Walker, 1990.
   Information about HIV and AIDS, how they are transmitted and the risk behaviors known as of the date of publication.

Johnson, Eric. *People, Love, Sex and Families.* Walker, 1985.
   Modern family situations are discussed, as well as sexual responsibility and related questions.

Landau, Elaine. *We Have AIDS.* Watts, 1990.
   Personal accounts of nine young people who have AIDS. Each account is followed by a brief "facts about AIDS" section which provides basic information.

Madaras, Lynda. *The "What's Happening to My Body?" Book for Girls.* (With Area Madaras.) New edition. Newmarket Press, 1988. *The "What's Happing to My Body?" Book for Boys.* (With Dane Saavedra.) New edition. Newmarket Press, 1988.

Direct, reassuring, and humorous; internal and external anatomy and development are discussed in detail. The book for girls has a chapter explaining what's happening to boys, while the book for boys explains female anatomy and development.

Madaras, Lynda. *Lynda Madaras Talks to Teens about AIDS: An Essential Guide for Parents, Teachers, and Young People.* Newmarket Press, 1988. Discusses what is currently known about AIDS, including guidelines for "safer sex" and how not to be embarrassed about it.

Nilsson, Lennart. *How Was I Born? Reproduction and Birth for Children.* Delacorte, 1975.
Remarkable in-utero photographs show the stage-by-stage development of the fetus, up to and including birth.

Parrot, Andrea. *Coping with Date Rape and Acquaintance Rape.* Rosen Publishing Group, 1988.
Defines and discusses date rape, including the communications gap often existing between teen males and females, and commonly held myths about behavior and implied consent. Discusses how to find counseling and related topics.

Rench, Janice E. *Understanding Sexual Identity: A Book for Gay Teens and Their Friends.* Lerner, 1990.
This book is designed to answer the questions of young teenagers attempting to understand gay identity, their own or that of their relatives or friends.

Terkel, Susan & Janice E. Rench. *Feeling Safe, Feeling Strong: How to Avoid Sexual Abuse and What to Do If It Happens to You.* Lerner, 1984.
How to say "no" effectively and what to do if "no" doesn't work. Where to go for help.

Selected and annotated by Marian Drabkin,
Librarian, Lawrence Hall of Science,
University of California, Berkeley.

Index